# Bert and the Magic Lamp
## and Other Good-Night Stories

By Michaela Muntean
Illustrated by Tom Cooke

**A SESAME STREET / GOLDEN PRESS BOOK**
Published by Western Publishing Company, Inc., Racine, Wisconsin 53404

# BERT AND THE MAGIC LAMP

"Hey, Bert," said Ernie as he came running through the front door of their apartment, "look what I found!"

Ernie held up an old brass lamp covered with dust.

"Oh, Ernie," said Bert, "why do you keep bringing home that kind of junk?"

"Junk?" cried Ernie. "Bert, old buddy, this is a treasure! When I get back from riding my bike, the first thing I'm going to do is polish this lamp. Then you'll see!"

So Ernie went out to ride his bike, and Bert went back to his reading. When Bert had finished his magazine, he looked up and saw the old lamp Ernie had left on the kitchen table.

"Ernie will never clean that lamp," he said. "It will only sit around collecting more dust. Then Ernie will put it in the closet. Then one day someone will open the closet and the lamp will fall and hit that person on the head, and that person will probably be me."

Bert sighed. He could picture the whole thing. "I might as well polish this lamp myself and see what it looks like. If it looks nice, we'll keep it. If not, out it goes."

So Bert got a rag and began to rub the lamp. Suddenly there was a loud *KERPOOF!* and a genie appeared.

"Thanks for letting me out," said the genie. "No one has rubbed that lamp for years. You can't imagine how cramped and stuffy it is in there. You don't mind if I do a few exercises to loosen up, do you?"

Bert didn't know what to say as he watched the genie.

"Aah! I feel much better," said the genie when he had finished his exercises. "Now we can get down to business. What do you wish?"

"What do you mean?" asked Bert.

"I mean what do you wish for?" repeated the genie. "Haven't you ever heard of the genie in the magic lamp?"

"Of course I have," said Bert. "But that was in a storybook about a boy named Aladdin."

"I remember him," said the genie. "Small guy with lots of wishes."

Bert thought for a minute. "How about a nice big bowl of oatmeal?"

"That's an easy one," said the genie, and a bowl of steaming oatmeal suddenly appeared on the table.

When Bert had finished eating his oatmeal, the genie asked him for his next wish.

Bert looked down at his brown-and-white saddle shoes. "I could use a new pair of shoelaces," he said. And in a flash there was a new pair of brown laces on Bert's shoes.

"I hope you don't mind my saying this," said the genie, "but these are some of the dullest wishes I have ever heard. Wouldn't you like a castle, or a princess to fall in love with, or chests filled with gold and precious jewels?"

"No," said Bert. "I don't think I would." But to make the genie feel better, he wished for a new pigeon cage.

Just then Bert heard Ernie coming up the stairs.

"Say, Mr. Genie, please get back inside the lamp now," Bert whispered, and the genie disappeared.

"Hey, Bert," said Ernie as he came into the room, "where did you get that new pigeon cage?"

Bert shrugged. "Oh, it just kind of appeared," he said.

Then Ernie noticed the lamp. "I told you that old lamp would look great when it was polished. And look what else I found—a great old carpet! When I get back from roller-skating, I'll vacuum it."

When Ernie had gone, Bert looked at the carpet and sighed. "Well," he said, "you never know what could happen," and he went to get the vacuum cleaner.

# LIFE-STYLES OF THE LARGE AND FURRY

Welcome to "Life-styles of the Large and Furry"! We are here at 456 Snuffle Circle to visit the Snuffleupagus family at home. We have just knocked on the door of their attractive cave, and Mrs. Snuffleupagus has been kind enough to invite us inside. It is true that from the outside a cave looks rather bumpy and stony, but inside you will be surprised to see how warm and cozy a cave can be.

Mrs. Snuffleupagus has to go to her exercise class, so her son, Snuffy, and her daughter, Alice, have offered to give us a tour of their cave home.

The first room Snuffy shows us is the living room. It has big comfortable chairs and a little fireplace. On the ceiling is a lovely layer of moss, which gives the room a soft green glow. We ask Snuffy about this, and he says that Snuffleupaguses like to eat moss for a snack, so it is very convenient to have it growing on their ceilings. Since you are probably not a Snuffleupagus, this might not seem as exciting to you as it does to Snuffy and his family.

Next we visit the kitchen, where we find Mr. Snuffleupagus boiling cabbage and cooking spaghetti. Snuffy and Alice tell us that these are their favorite foods. Their daddy is making extra-large portions because Snuffy's friend Big Bird is coming to dinner tonight.

In Alice's bedroom, she shows us her bed, which is like a big cubbyhole cut into the side of the cave. It is lined with straw and then covered with soft blankets.

Snuffy's bedroom is next to Alice's. His bed is made the same way, but it is much bigger because he is a much bigger Snuffleupagus. On his bed there are two pillows. One is for his head, and the other is for his snuffle.

Next to the bedrooms is a part of the cave that has a little stream running through it. This is where the Snuffleupaguses take their baths. Alice shows us how she can blow bubbles in the water with her snuffle. She says that her big brother, Snuffy, taught her how, and we all agree that Alice is one of the best snuffle-bubble blowers we have ever seen.

The Snuffleupaguses tell us that one of the nicest things about cave life is that most caves are connected to other caves. This makes it very easy to visit neighbors. Snuffy leads us down a long tunnel, and we arrive at the cave of Aunt Agnes Snuffleupagus.

She is very friendly and offers everyone moss-cream cupcakes. Unfortunately, I have just finished lunch so I am not hungry, but everyone else seems to enjoy them.

Farther down the cave-block live the Count's bats. We want to interview them, but it is very difficult to have a conversation with them while they are hanging upside down.

That's all we have time for today, but please join us next time, when we will explore the life-styles of the small and fluffy!

# THE SHADOW-PICTURE SHOW

There was a full moon in the sky and moonlight shone through
the window of Ernie and Bert's bedroom. Ernie could not go to
sleep. The brightness of the moon cast shadows on the wall and
ceiling. Ernie held up his hand. He could see its shadow clearly on
the wall. Then he held up his foot and wiggled his toes. His toes'
shadow wiggled back from the ceiling. Then Ernie held up Rubber
Duckie. He moved the duckie back and forth, and the shadow
looked like Rubber Duckie was swimming on the ceiling. That gave
Ernie an idea.

He hopped out of bed and opened the closet.

"I'll need this, and that…" Ernie said as things clattered and crashed around him.

Bert opened one eye. "Ernie," he said sleepily, "what are you doing?"

"I'm going to tell you a story that will help you get to sleep," Ernie said.

"But, Ernie," Bert groaned, "I *am* asleep."

"Gee, Bert," said Ernie, "you don't *sound* like you're asleep."

Bert groaned again. By now he had opened both eyes.

Ernie climbed back into bed carrying an armload of stuff.

"I know you're going to like this, Bert," said Ernie. "Just look at the ceiling and tell me what you see."

"I see the shadow of Rubber Duckie," Bert said with a yawn.

"Right," said Ernie. "He was swimming on the Ceiling Sea when he met a big beach ball." Ernie held up his baseball. "The beach ball asked Rubber Duckie if he would like to go on an ocean adventure, and Rubber Duckie said he would. So off they went together. Suddenly there was a big wave— *WHOOSH!*—and the beach ball got swept away by the tide.

"Now, who do you think Rubber Duckie met next?" Ernie asked.
"It looks like the shadow of your baseball mitt," Bert said.
"No," said Ernie, "it's a giant seashell, and the seashell introduced Rubber Duckie to his friend the sea serpent."

Ernie took off his baseball mitt and slipped his hand inside a sock and held it up toward the ceiling. Its shadow looked just like a sea serpent.

"Don't worry," Ernie said to Bert, "this is a friendly sea serpent. He just told Rubber Duckie that there is a big storm on the way and he's going to show him a safe place to hide until it is over."

By now Ernie's arms were getting tired, so he lowered them to rest a minute. He was also beginning to feel a little sleepy, so he closed his eyes.

"Well?" said Bert eagerly. "Then what happened?" But the only answer he heard was the sound of Ernie's snoring.

Bert sighed and got out of bed. He carefully pulled the sock off Ernie's hand and put it on his own. He picked up the baseball, the mitt, and Rubber Duckie. Then he climbed back into bed.

Bert was wide awake. He lay in bed, looking up at the shadows of Rubber Duckie and the sea serpent on the ceiling.

"So," he began, "the sea serpent took Rubber Duckie to a quiet cove while the storm raged and crashed around them...."